The Warriors

by Joseph Bruchac

Carolrhoda Books • Minneapolis

For my Iroquois friends,
especially Rick Hill, Oren Lyons, and Peter Jemison,
whose hearts are always in the game.

Carolrhoda Books
A division of Lerner Publishing Group, Inc.
241 First Avenue North
Minneapolis, MN 55401 USA

For reading levels and more information, look up this title at www.lernerbooks.com.

Cataloging-in-Publication Data

Bruchac, Joseph, 1942–
     The Warriors / by Joseph Bruchac.
         p.   cm.
     Summary: Jake has left the reservation for Weltimore Academy and entered a different world. Everyone there loves lacrosse, but no one understands it the way Jake does, as an Iroquois. And no one understands Jake either.
     ISBN-13: 978-1-58196-002-0 (lib. bdg. : alk. paper)
     ISBN-13: 978-1-58196-022-8 (pbk. : alk. paper)
     ISBN-13: 978-0-7613-8277-5 (EB pdf)
     1. Lacrosse—Juvenile fiction. 2. Iroquois Indians—Juvenile fiction. 3. Boarding school students—Juvenile fiction. [1. Lacrosse—Fiction. 2. Iroquois Indians—Fiction. 3. Boarding school students—Fiction.]
     PZ7.B82816Wa 2003 [Fic] dc22
     OCLC: 52607278

Manufactured in the United States of America
14-48531-7788-10/1/2019

TABLE OF CONTENTS

CHAPTER ONE ~ In the Box 5

CHAPTER TWO ~ The Creator's Game 15

CHAPTER THREE ~ The Drumbeat 21

CHAPTER FOUR ~ Deer Run 27

CHAPTER FIVE ~ Weltimore 37

CHAPTER SIX ~ The Cabinet 49

CHAPTER SEVEN ~ Her Decision 61

CHAPTER EIGHT ~ Drills 67

CHAPTER NINE ~ Another Day 77

CHAPTER TEN ~ Coach Scott's Story 83

CHAPTER ELEVEN ~ Game Day 89

CHAPTER TWELVE ~ Running Home 95

CHAPTER THIRTEEN ~ Shot 103

CHAPTER FOURTEEN ~ Secure 107

CHAPTER FIFTEEN ~ All Play 117

CHAPTER SIXTEEN ~ A Warrior's Home 123

CHAPTER ONE

IN THE BOX

J AKE LOOKED UP at the sun in the afternoon sky. It shone right in his face this final quarter of the game, but he didn't mind.

"Elder Brother," he said in a soft voice, using the old Iroquois name for the sun, He Who Loves to Watch the People Play, "I thank you for looking at me."

The sun was not the only one looking at Jake and the other teenage lacrosse players. Hundreds of Iroquois people had gathered around the wooden walls of the reservation's new box lacrosse field. It wasn't just the population of the rez. Lined up beyond the field were the cars, vans, and pick-ups that had brought the Tuscarora team and its crowd of fans. Whether it was an adult or junior league game, like the one Jake was playing, boxla drew everyone in like noisy bees around a hive.

Today the buzz was especially intense. Both teams

facing off had gone unbeaten until this final game of their summer season. Today's game would settle who was the best team: the Tuskies or Jake's team, the Junior Warriors.

Almost all of Jake's close relatives were in the crowd. He lifted his head to look over at them. His aunt and uncle, his younger cousins. They were there. But *she* wasn't. Grampa Sky was, though. Like always, his grandfather knew when Jake was looking at him. Grampa Sky lifted his hand and put it against his chest, making the gesture Jake knew was just for him.

Jake thought for a minute about the stories Grampa Sky told him about how it was before Europeans came. Back then, lacrosse was played without walls or boundaries on the fields. Back then, just about everyone, young or old, would have had a lacrosse stick in his hands, playing one village against the other. Now, though, this favorite Iroquois game was played on a field closed in by wooden walls like those of the Canadian indoor rinks, where box lacrosse had first been played in the 1920s during the hockey off-season.

Jake shook his head. It was good to remember the

stories, but right now he had to keep his mind on the game. He looked quickly around the field, checking the positions of the other six men on his team, especially Frank Tarbell and Rick Jamieson. It was easy to pick Frank out, off to his left, even without seeing the number on his jersey. In August, Frank had dyed his normally jet-black hair bright red. From under his helmet, Frank's ponytail hung down his back like a crimson flag. Rick was just as easy to spot. His long, lean arms and legs made him stand out like a heron in a pond.

First Frank, then Rick, raised a hand to wave in Jake's direction. Jake raised a hand back to them. He knew they would try to get the ball to him for one last shot.

Jake pulled in his chin and pushed out his lower lip. Anyone who knew him knew what that meant. His father had called it "Jake's buffalo look." Nothing was going to push him back. Two minutes to go. The Junior Warriors were behind by one score. Seven to six. Crunch time.

Thirty yards downfield the player opposite Frank scooped up the ball without breaking stride. Driving hard, he planted his left foot and then rolled his right leg back, using his body as a shield. It was the kind of change-of-direction dodge a lax kid did twenty times every day in drills. Frank should have had no trouble with it. But his foot caught on a loose piece of turf. He stumbled and lost the ball. It bounced once and then the Tuscarora boy with the number ten on his jersey caught it in the mesh pocket of his lacrosse stick.

Now Rick was the defenseman in front of Ten. He swung his long stick across one-handed. The wrap check failed as Ten lowered his own stick, ducked under, and whipped a perfect sidearm pass. The lacrosse ball flew as fast as a diving hawk across the field.

It was such a good pass that the Tuscarora midfielder, number seven, smiled as he got ready to catch it. Jake and his teammates had nicknamed this player Sunscreen. That was the way it went in an Iroquois lacrosse game, always teasing the other players, talking good-natured trash at them. Tuscaroras tended to be lighter-skinned than other Iroquois people, so their game names reflected it. Ten was Freckles. Eleven was Beachboy.

Jake saw Sunscreen's smile. It was the same smile that Jake had noticed on the midfielder's face when he'd scored the goal that put the Warriors down by one point.

Jake knew what Sunscreen was thinking: that there was no way Jake could get to that pass before he did. In his own mind, Sunscreen was already twenty yards up the field, dodging defenders, set for the overhand shot that would ice the Tuskies' victory.

Jake lowered his stick and let his shoulders slump as if he were giving up, knowing that Sunscreen would see him. It was one of the tricks Uncle Irwin had taught him. "You win with your mind as much as you win with your body, Jake. Never let the other side know what you are really thinking."

The ball thumped into the pocket of Sunscreen's stick. He lowered it into the box, then pivoted to go around Jake. But Jake wasn't there. Just as the ball had reached the Tuscarora player, Jake had raced behind him. With a perfect poke check, Jake thrust his stick against Sunscreen's gloved lower hand. The ball popped out of the webbing, and Jake snagged it in midair.

Jake whipped past one midfielder, then bull-dodged between two defenders. The goalie was waiting in a crouch, his webbed stick looking as wide as a fish net. He was set to block the overhand shot most midfielders would have tried.

Jake was not most midfielders. He was Eddie Forrest's son. As he reached the edge of the crease and he saw the goalie start to follow him across, Jake suddenly planted his left foot, whipped the stick up, and shot the ball back-handed over his left shoulder. It bounced past the goalie's feet and into the net, just a heartbeat before the sound of the referee's whistle ending the game. Seven-seven. A tie.

A shout went up from the crowd on both sides of the field, the same way it almost always did at the end of a game between Indians. It didn't matter much which side scored the most points; it was the beauty of the game that mattered, the way it brought people's minds and hearts together. Both sides had played well. Ending in a tie only made it better.

"Hey, Buffalo Burger!" someone shouted.

Jake turned around, knowing that shout was for him. That was the nickname the Tusky kids had given him. One of them had recognized him from the Green Corn Festival last summer when Jake had helped his Uncle Irwin run the snack bar tent. They sold traditional Indian Pow Wow foods. Buffalo Burger. It could have been worse. They might have called him Corn Soup.

It was Tusky Seven. Sunscreen. A big grin appeared on his wide face. He had his right hand held up in front of him as he approached.

"Buff-a-lo Bur-ger Boy!" he said, as he slapped Jake's palm.

Jake grinned back. "Sun-screen Kid," he said.

They switched their hand slap into an Indian power handshake. Between the two of them, they had scored more than half of all the goals that afternoon.

"Pete Hall," Sunscreen said, tapping his chest with his left hand as he held onto Jake's wrist with his right. "My dad is that Indian artist, you know the one. You even got one of his pieces here in your school, you know, eh?"

Jake nodded. "Jake Forrest. My dad—" He paused, not sure what he was about to say or why he had started to say it. His dad was dead, had been dead since Jake was seven. Killed when some scaffolding came down on him while he was working iron in Montreal.

Jake nodded. "See ya, Sun Kid. *Oneh.*"

"*Oneh.*"

The other members of Jake's team came up to congratulate him, just as the coaches were calling for the sides to line up. The two teams shook hands, laughing about the tie.

It's over, Jake thought, the thrill of the game leaving him. *It's all over.*

Usually a social and a feast would have been shared by both sides, but the buses had had some kind of problem, so they had to have them back before dark. The Tuscarora Junior Eagles and their coaches couldn't stick around, but every kid, coach, and helper was given a paper bag filled with fry bread and a cup of corn soup prepared by the mothers of the Junior Warriors to enjoy on their ride home. Portable hospitality was better than none at all. A social would still take place for those who had driven their cars all the way from the Tuscarora Reservation near Niagara Falls to be at the game. Family and lacrosse and sharing—they were the heart of being Iroquois.

Jake sat down on the side of the field, his helmet and gloves on his right side, his beloved wooden stick on his left. The crowd had moved up to the longhouse for the social. No one else was around.

Why is this happening? Why do I have to go off to Maryland? Why do I have to leave the reservation, leave all my friends and family? This is my land. It's the only place I've ever lived.

The reservation was a place where just about everyone else was Indian and Jake could just be himself. The condo where he'd be living with his mom was far from home. In so many ways.

"What am I going to do?" he softly said aloud to himself. "Nobody is going to know me there. Nobody."

CHAPTER TWO

THE CREATOR'S GAME

"JAKE," A DEEP VOICE RUMBLED. It was a voice that Jake loved more than any other voice in the world. He remembered how, when he was little, that voice had sung him lullabies in his people's language. Those were times when his mom was off at school and his dad was working iron somewhere far away. It was the voice of Uncle Irwin, his mom's brother. Uncle Irwin and his wife Aunt Alice had babysat for Jake so much, it was like Jake was just another one of their kids.

"Jake?" the voice repeated.

Jake didn't look up. "Hi, Uncle Irwin," he said.

Irwin Printup folded himself down into a sitting position in one easy motion. Even though he was as big as a bear now, he still could move almost as gracefully as when he'd been the best attacker on the Syracuse lax squad—the one that won the Nationals two years running.

They both looked out over the field. Seven generations of players from their reservation had battled on that ground. Sons, father, grandfathers . . . the same names and numbers repeated from one generation to the next, lacrosse warriors whose sweat and tears and blood had made the soil of their reservation even more sacred.

The sun was about to vanish behind the pines on the high hill to the west. Neither of them said anything, but both Jake and his uncle looked toward the sunset, their minds connecting as one: *Let us be thankful that we were given this day.*

"I think we pleased the Creator with this game," Uncle Irwin rumbled.

Jake nodded. Lacrosse was the Creator's Game. It was a gift that the Holder Up of the Heavens had given the Iroquois people, a way to make them strong, a way to join together in a great game that was also a prayer. That was why they still sometimes played the medicine game form of lacrosse here and in other Iroquois communities, dedicating the game to someone who was ill in the hopes that the spirit of the game would help the sick person recover.

Irwin Printup put one hand on his nephew's shoulder, the powerful muscle tense and strong. Even though Jake was only twelve, he was almost as strong as a man. Jake's uncle moved his other hand over and began to massage Jake's neck and shoulders, loosening the tightness.

"Uncle Irwin," Jake said. Then he stopped.

"I know," Uncle Irwin said. "You don't want to go."

Jake twisted around to look up at his uncle. Then he turned his eyes back to the ground.

"Why can't I stay here with you and Aunt Alice?" Jake asked.

Irwin Printup shook his head. "Your mom loves you," he said. "That's why. She figures you and she have spent too much time apart, what with her being off at school so much, getting her law degree. Now that she can afford a place big enough for you both, as well as having enough to pay your tuition, she just wants you with her."

Jake couldn't stop himself. Even though he knew the words were selfish, they jumped out of his mouth. "What about what *I* want?"

Uncle Irwin took his hands off Jake's shoulders. "You know," he said, "when your great-grandfather got sent off to Carlisle Indian School, all the way down to Pennsylvania, his mother cried. That was back in 1912. She didn't know if she was ever going to see him again. But he found his way back here, Jake. And that is the way it has always been. Our people find a way to get back."

Jake squared his shoulders. Uncle Irwin was always like that, able to find the right words to say. That was one of the reasons the Clan Mothers of their reservation had chosen Irwin Printup to be a Faith Keeper, one whose job it was to keep their old ways alive, to protect the heart of their culture.

Jake picked up his lacrosse stick and placed it in his uncle's hands. "I want you to hold on to this for me," Jake said.

Irwin Printup cradled the stick. He knew that it belonged in his nephew's hands, but he understood what Jake was doing. A stick became part of a man, an extension of his eyes and hands and heart. "I'll take care of it," he said. "Now here comes your aunt. Bet she's wondering why we aren't up there getting our share of fry bread."

Jake and Uncle Irwin stood and walked up the hill

toward Aunt Alice. As always, a big smile lit up her face. Aunt Alice was one of those people whose happy face held a smile the way the sky holds the morning sun. But now her smile seemed even brighter than usual.

"Jake," she said, "someone's waiting for you up at the longhouse. Your mom is here."

"Did she see me play?" Jake asked. "I never noticed her in the—"

Aunt Alice's smile dimmed. "No, honey. She thought she had it planned just right to get here in time. But you know how it is with flights out of Washington. She had a two-hour delay, so she just got here."

Jake's shoulders slumped. "I've got to put my stuff away first," he said. He dragged his feet as he headed for the back door of the school.

CHAPTER THREE

THE DRUMBEAT

JAKE SLOWLY PUT AWAY HIS GEAR in the school locker room. He was in no hurry to get to the social where his mom was waiting. Usually he'd be running as fast as he could to get to her, to feel her strong arms wrap around him, to hear her whisper "Jakey" into his hair. It didn't matter that he was taller than she was now. Whenever Mom showed up, he turned back into the little kid who just couldn't be hugged long enough.

Today was different. Even though it had been two weeks since he'd seen her, Jake wasn't eager this time to have her pull him close. He knew this time she was going to say it was time for him to go.

Jake shook his head. He realized he was feeling sorry for himself. Nothing good ever came of that. He had learned that a man had to keep a good mind if he hoped to accomplish anything. Otherwise a person could become angry and confused, and his path would be just as twisted as his thoughts. That was what Grampa Sky had told him more than once. Grampa Sky always seemed to have a story to tell or a wise word that helped Jake understand the best way to go.

Grampa Sky had made Jake's favorite lacrosse stick, the one he had just placed in Uncle Irwin's care. According to how white people reckoned things, Grampa Sky wasn't really his grandfather, but something more along the lines of a great-uncle, two times removed. But he was still Grampa Sky to Jake and to most of the other kids. On this reservation, the web of connections among families went back hundreds of years, and everyone knew exactly how he or she was related to everyone else. Grampa Sky was also a member of the Wolf Clan, just as Jake and his mother were. That gave them an even more special relationship.

Jake had watched for Grampa Sky at the game. When he scored the final goal, Grampa Sky was the first person Jake saw, standing up with his right hand on his heart and his eyes locked on Jake. Jake's heart had swelled with pride just then. Now he had let himself get depressed.

Jake closed the locker door. He slipped his feet into

his sneakers and pulled on the T-shirt with a picture of Litefoot, the Iroquois rapper. Jake clipped his Walkman to his belt, slipped the earphones onto his head, and stood up. It was time to go see his mom.

As Jake walked out the back door, a tall figure walked out from behind the maple tree. Jake stepped back in surprise. It seemed as if the tall old man had been a part of the tree and was emerging from it.

"Grampa Sky," Jake said, "I didn't see you there."

Grampa Sky's leathery face opened up into a smile. "Old Indian trick," he said. "You know that story about the lacrosse game and the maple tree, don't you? Seems there was this boy who was always bullying everyone else when they played lacrosse. He was a real good player, but that wasn't enough for him. He thought he had to be the best. So he'd always play with the smaller boys. That way he could just push them around. The elders warned him not to act that way, but he didn't listen. Finally, one of the old men, one who had power, picked that boy up and shoved him into a maple tree. That tree just opened up as he went in and then closed around him so that his head stuck out one side, and his feet stuck out the other side. They left him there like that all day. Finally, just before the sun went down, that old man pulled him out of the tree. From then on, that boy didn't bully anyone."

"I see," Jake said. He understood what Grampa Sky was saying. His story was meant to both praise Jake for being the best player on the field that day and to remind him to stay humble.

Grampa Sky reached out to take Jake's hand. He gently shook it. "*Niaweh skanoh*, grandchild. Good game you played there."

"*Niaweh*," Jake said. Grampa Sky's hand was rough and cool in his grasp. He wanted to keep holding onto it, as if it would keep him from having to leave.

"Just wanted a minute to talk before we get up to the social," Grampa Sky said as they walked along. "It's hard to get a word in edgewise there."

Jake tried not to smile. Everyone respected Grampa Sky so much that any time he started to talk, they stopped so they could hear what he had to say.

Grampa Sky tapped his palm against Jake's chest. *Thump-thump, thump-thump.* The heartbeat rhythm. "You know that sound, Jake?"

Jake nodded. The drumbeat of the heart was the first sound each person heard. Even before you were born, you could hear the beating of your mother's heart.

Grampa Sky nodded. "Just keep listening," he said.

Neither one of them said anything more as they walked the rest of the way. Grampa Sky slipped away when they rounded the corner of the longhouse. Chairs and tables had been put out in the open area between the buildings.

Lots of people were there, but, as always, the first person Jake saw was his mother. She always stood out in a crowd, and not just because she was taller than many of the other women. There was always a sort of presence about his mom, the same kind of strength that Grampa Sky had, a self-assurance that made most people pay attention to her. It was only when she was around Jake that she seemed uncertain of what to say.

Is that because I haven't been listening? Jake wondered, thinking of Grampa Sky's advice.

She hadn't seen Jake yet because she was turned the other way. She had on her favorite denim jacket, the one with the shape of a Wolf, their clan animal, beaded on the back.

"Listen," Jake whispered to himself. "I have to listen."

Just then his mother turned around and saw him. Her face lit up in a smile, warmer than the sun that shone low in the late afternoon sky just behind her.

"I missed you," she said when he walked up to her. Then she hesitated, suddenly uncertain about whether or not to embrace him.

"I missed you, too, Mom," Jake said, wrapping his arms around her.

"Jakey," his mother said, pressing his head against her shoulder. From there, he could hear the drumming of her heart.

CHAPTER FOUR

DEER RUN

OO MUCH PAVEMENT. That was all he could think as he looked at the wide, empty, black road that curved through Deer Run.

Jake sat on the paved driveway next to the small patch of brilliant green that pretended to be a lawn in front of his mother's Maryland condo. It was grass all right, but Jake had never seen grass like this before. Every blade was neat and shiny and exactly the same height. But it shouldn't have been surprising.

After all, Jake thought, *they bring this stuff in rolls on the back of trucks.* Two days ago he'd watched—there'd been nothing else to do—while workers unrolled an instant lawn at the condo down the road. They pegged it in place, watered it, and then sprayed it with something that Jake suspected was deadly to all known life. They had taken down the little red plastic warning signs this afternoon, but Jake wasn't about to forget them. And he wasn't going to do any sunbathing lying out on their own so-called lawn. He didn't trust it. At least the asphalt was safer.

Jake picked up his skateboard, turned it upside down in his lap, and idly spun the wheels with his palm. Some kids might think this was skateboard heaven. Not a car to be seen. Nobody to tell you to get out of the road. No trucks throwing gravel up in your face like on the rez. And no other kids. There were no rules against having kids in Deer Run, but most of the people who lived in these units didn't have kids. If they did, they'd move to Upper Deer Run half a mile away.

The Upper Run offered each family six whole rooms instead of the four-and-a-half pre-fabricated cubicles (with attached private garage) like his mom's unit. Some kids in the Upper Run were probably his age, but his mom had told him that whatever new friends he would have here in Maryland, he'd most likely have to find at his new school. Right now, with everyone at work, even finding another living human being seemed unlikely.

It was weird. It was like one of those scenes in a science-fiction movie when someone wakes up to find out everyone else in the world has vanished and he's completely alone. All Jake had to do was look overhead to know that wasn't true. Air Force and commercial jets were constantly up there, criss-crossing back and forth, the highest ones leaving straight, white trails like lines of chalk drawn on the blue pavement of the sky.

Jake could also hear the neverending traffic. The sign by the gated entrance said that Deer Run was "a secluded escape from the busy world." But this commuters' community, where nobody knew anybody else and a mass exodus began every morning right at sunup, wasn't that isolated. Even at night Jake heard, and even felt, the rumble of trucks and cars on the big highway a mile away. Because of the street lights, the night sky was never really dark.

Jake spun the wheels of his skateboard again. Yesterday he had probably gone ten miles on it, up and down one little street after another, where just about every building looked the same. Only the numbers and the cute little names told him where he was. Cougar Court. Beaver Lane. Woodchuck Terrace. Moose Walk. As if any animal bigger than a fly could even get in here—and once inside find anything to eat besides the poisoned green grass and the neatly spaced little maple trees with withered leaves. *Deer Run,* Jake thought. *Good name. It's what any deer that finds itself here would do as fast as it could—run away.*

Jake picked up his skateboard. He walked to the side door, checked the numbers his mother had printed on his armband, and then keyed in the combination. He was careful to do it exactly right. The keypad was hooked up to the guard box at the gate of Deer Run. Yesterday, when he'd tried three times before hitting the right combination, the phone was already ringing when he stepped inside. It was security, checking to make sure an "unauthorized entry" had not occurred.

Jake looked at the cell phone on the table. It was his mom's spare, one of those miniature phones that he could clip on his belt. He'd used it almost all day the first day he was left here alone while Mom had to go in to her office. He'd called Uncle Irwin's mobile phone in his truck and Aunt Alice's bright yellow wall phone that hung in her kitchen. He'd called Grampa Sky's old black phone that sat on the table in the entry room to their old house, the room that Grampa Sky called the mudroom. He had even reached his best buddy Rick Jamieson, catching him at home just before he went out to the lacrosse box to do shooting drills like "Around the World" with the rest of the team. It was like magic that day. Every number he called, the person always answered on the first ring and was really glad to hear from him. Jake talked and talked. As soon as one conversation was over, he punched in another number and hit the green SEND button. He couldn't remember much of what he said to anyone, but he knew he still had more to say.

After talking to everyone whose number he could remember, he started the round of calls again. The tone in Uncle Irwin's voice changed the third time he answered his mobile phone and heard Jake's voice saying, "Hey, Uncle Irwin. It's me. What's up?"

"Jake," Uncle Irwin said, "I love to hear from you, but I think you need to be where you are, nephew. You can't live inside a phone."

Now remembering yesterday's embarrassing phone lesson, Jake slumped into the family room and collapsed onto the Mad Scientist Chair in front of the TV. He'd given it that name because even though it was cushioned and comfortable to sit in, it was all strange angles. It had this control box you could use to make it change shapes. It could go up and down, recline, and lift back up again. With his eyes closed and the MSC reclined, Jake could imagine himself being lifted up toward the roof that would swing open so the lightning bolt could come down and strike him, just like in *Frankenstein*.

Jake picked up the remote, but he didn't turn on the giant home entertainment system. Instead he closed his eyes and held his hands in front of him, trying to imagine the feel of his lacrosse stick, the scent of the field behind the Nation School, the sound of a yellow-bellied sapsucker drumming against the big hollow oak tree in the woods behind the sunrise edge of the field.

Then he sighed and opened his eyes. This was his last day here. Tomorrow was the start of school. He'd be out there at the gatehouse, wearing his new school blazer, waiting to be picked up by the private bus at 6:28 A.M. for Weltimore Academy. He thought maybe he should turn on the bigger-than-a-drive-in-movie-screen TV and take advantage of the 23 million different cable stations.

But Jake didn't turn on the TV. It didn't interest him. It was funny—that was how he felt about everything right now. Not happy, not sad, just not interested. It was sort of like this was all happening to someone else.

It was funny, too, how happy his mom was about everything. She was ecstatic about her job, about this condo—which she said was the first place she'd ever owned. She was delighted—she said—to have Jake with her.

Jake kind of liked being with her, too, but so far it hadn't felt real to him. It had been more like a vacation with a friendly stranger who looked like someone you used to know really well. Plus, even though his mom had intended to be with him pretty much 24/7 until he started school, things had come up at her job and she'd had to go to work, even though she supposedly had the whole week off. So Jake and his mom hadn't spent much time together, except evenings when she just talked nonstop about her job while Jake mostly said, "Unh-hunh."

At least I'm making her happy by being here, he thought. *I suppose I should at least be glad of that.*

She seemed especially happy about the way Jake took her big decision about what he *couldn't* do. Jake remembered the scene back at the social. After hugging him and telling him how much he'd grown, his mom had taken him outside onto the back steps and sat down beside him. She told him how important this opportunity was for him. Going to this new school would open doors for him, taking him where the other Indian kids at the rez wouldn't have a chance to go. He could get the kind of education that would make it possible for him to do great things for his people. That was what she had done, she told him, and she'd had to make sacrifices, too.

She'd been nervous. Jake knew because she kept touching her left earring while she was talking. He had first noticed her special sign of nervousness when he was a very little kid. She had been doing it more often since his dad had died.

"Jake," she had said that day, "I have something really important to tell you."

"Unh-hunh," Jake said. "Unh-hunh" was his all-purpose reply to grown-ups and friends alike. He had worked on it so much that he guessed he had more than twenty different ways to say it. This particular "unh-hunh" was the bright, attentive, I-am-really-listening-to-you one, always accompanied by brief eye contact and a nod of the head.

His mom rubbed at her earring. "Jake . . . ," she said again.

"Unh-hunh," he answered, meaning something along the lines of "Yup, you guessed it. That's who I am."

"Jake, your teachers here all say that you are not working up to your ability. I think that's because you need to focus. Weltimore has the highest academic requirements. I was lucky to get you in. They had an opening at the very last minute. You are going to have to work extra-hard, son."

"Unh, hunnh." Saying it just a little slower this way meant Jake knew something was coming that he wasn't going to like.

"Jake, you know what they say about us."

Jake knew. He'd heard it often enough from his mother to know that the word "us" meant all Indians, just as "they" meant the white people who thought Indians were nothing more than lazy bums and ignorant savages. His mom had felt so much hurt when she was in school and discovered that some people thought of her in that way. Because of this, Jake knew that his mom was determined to be not only as good as a white lawyer, but even better than any of them. He also knew that saying "unh-hunh" would not satisfy his mother this time.

"I know, Mom," he said.

Jake's mom looked at him. "Then you will understand why I have decided that you will have to give up something you love."

She looked intently at him. Jake kept his gaze toward the ground, limiting any sign of emotion on his face, as he thought, *Only one thing? I thought you were already asking me to give up my whole life here.*

His mom took a deep breath. "Jake," she said, her voice taking on a business-like tone, "I am going to ask you to promise—just for this first term—not to play lacrosse."

She looked hard at her son, expecting to see his defiant "buffalo look."

Instead, and without hesitation, Jake held out his hand to her. "I promise, Mom," he said.

CHAPTER FIVE
WELTIMORE

THE OTHER KIDS ON THE BUS were talking to each other, but Jake, who was way in the back, wasn't listening. For now, at least, they didn't seem to even see him. He hadn't moved his backpack off the seat next to him when other kids started getting on the bus. He just kept staring out the window. They'd taken the hint: Leave the new kid alone.

The bus wasn't much bigger than a van, two-thirds the size of one of the "June Bugs." That was what the kids back on the rez called the four buses in the orange fleet that served the Nation School. Jake had never had to take a bus before, living only two hundred yards down the road from the school. But it was different here. Deer Run was three miles away from Weltimore. Even if he'd wanted to go that distance on foot, the crazy maze of highways and streets that the bus negotiated would have made it impossible. Close as it was, with the nineteen stops to pick up the thirty-one other boys who rode the bus, with all the merges and stoplights, and so many turns that Jake thought they were going to meet themselves coming and going, it took more than half an hour to reach the tree-lined entrance to his new school.

Jake saw right away that the trees were all maples. Jake loved maples. He remembered his uncle telling him about how the maple became the leader of the trees. It was the first tree to offer its gift to the people each year, giving its annual harvest of syrup. Just seeing the trees made him think of the late-winter smell of maple sap cooking down in the sugaring house behind the Nation School.

Then Jake noticed something. The Weltimore maples were different from the ones back on the rez. They had no broken branches, no dead limbs, no small marks on the sides left by decades of tapping. These trees looked like pictures of maples, perfect models instead of the real thing. Every one of the trees was exactly the same, pruned into conformity. They were as alike as every boy on the bus, all wearing the same school uniform.

Jake looked further out the window, past the perfect

maples. The drive led half a mile uphill to the impressive stone facade of Weltimore's main building. Jake rubbed his hands together. It wasn't really hot on the bus, but for some reason his palms were all sweaty. He started to wipe them on his legs, and then stopped. He didn't want to stain his new gray slacks or make a moist spot on them. He looked around and then pulled a handkerchief out of the side pocket of his backpack to dry his hands.

The driveway was long, but it wasn't long enough for Jake. He hoped it would go on forever so he wouldn't have to get out and go into that building. He'd never gone to a school where he didn't know anyone. That morning, his mom told him she had faith in his "adaptability." He'd just said, "Unh-hunh," and nodded. But after he'd looked the word up in his dictionary, he decided he'd agreed too soon. He doubted that he could "adjust, accommodate, or conform to new surroundings." In fact, he was sure he couldn't.

"Come on, son," the gray-uniformed bus driver said. His voice had some kind of deep southern accent that Jake had never heard before. Jake could see the man's dark face smiling at him in the big rearview mirror. "Summer's over," the man said, laughing. "Get on in there."

Jake walked down the aisle. His backpack caught on one seat after another as he walked, as if it didn't want to get off the bus, either. But a bell was ringing from somewhere inside the building, and Jake knew that, bad as it was, it would be much worse if he were late.

He jumped out of the bus and ran up the steps toward the door where the last of the other kids had just disappeared inside. He noticed something that made him pause for a moment before going inside, something that was carved into the stone at the right side of the door. It looked like an engraving of two lacrosse sticks.

He stepped through the door into a lobby with a ceiling so high that one of the tall maples along the driveway would hardly have touched it.

"Backpack and ID," a voice to his left said. Jake pulled his eyes away from the lobby ceiling. A tall man stood there holding out his right hand. The man had on a blue uniform with his name on a tag above the left pocket. *THOMAS*, it read.

Jake fumbled in his jacket pocket for the laminated ID card that his mother had given him. It hung from a red cord so he could wear it around his neck, but Jake had been too embarrassed to put it on.

The man took the card, looked at it, looked at Jake, and then nodded. He leaned down and used both hands to place the cord around Jake's neck.

"Supposed to wear that when y'all are on campus, Mr. For-rest," the man drawled. Then he placed the back-pack on a small conveyer belt that ran through a detec-tor of some kind. The man looked at a TV monitor and nodded. "Your turn, Mr. Forrest," he said.

Jake stood there in confusion. The other boys had all vanished from the lobby. He hadn't seen what they'd done. He didn't understand what the man named Thomas expected him to do now. Jake wondered, too, why Thomas, a grown man, had his first name on his badge while he called Jake, a kid, "Mr. Forrest." Jake looked at the conveyor belt. Was he supposed to lie down on it?

Thomas took him by the shoulder and gently steered him toward an open white plastic doorway. "Through there, just like in the airport," Thomas said. "You know the drill."

"I never—" Jake started to say. Then he choked off his words. He was probably the only kid in the whole school who had never been on an airplane. But with all the stuff that had been on the news over the last couple of years, he realized that he knew what he was supposed to do. Jake searched his pockets for metal of any kind, pulling out his house key and two quarters, which he dropped into a tray Thomas held out. Jake walked through the white plastic doorway. On the other side Thomas handed him his backpack, his change, and his keys. The look on Thomas's face was a little different now. He seemed a little less bored, a little more sympathetic.

"Go on," Thomas said. "You're going to do just fine here. New student check-in down there to the left. You see that sign there? Says 'Guidance'?"

Jake started down the hall. As he walked, he noticed a trophy case on the wall about fifty feet ahead. He wasn't close enough or at the right angle to see into it fully, but his heart began to beat a little faster when he thought he saw some rawhide webbing.

"Mr. For-rest," Thomas called to him.

Jake looked back.

Thomas motioned for him to come back.

"Forgot to tell you. Y'all are supposed to report to the Headmaster's office. Third door, down there on the right."

❧ ❧ ❧ ❧ ❧

A red-haired woman sat at a desk just inside the open door. She was listening to one of those telephone headsets that looked like something Jake had seen country western musicians wear at big concerts on TV. She peered over the top of her glasses at Jake. Then she held up the oversized green pencil in her left hand, motioning with it for Jake to enter, move right, sit, wait.

"Excellent," she said into her headset. "Good-bye. And you are?"

Jake realized she was talking to him now. "Me?" he asked.

The woman with the glasses and headset nodded. "Yes, I'm sure you are," she said, "but I also would like to know your name, young man."

She pointed her giant green pencil at the ID that was only partially visible because Jake had tucked it out of sight inside his jacket.

Jake pulled out the card and looked at it. Why was he

doing that? He knew his own name. He felt like an idiot.

"Jake Forrest," he mumbled.

The woman nodded again. "Thank you," she said. She looked down at a sheet of paper on her desk, and then raised her pencil again like a baton to point it at the open door behind her.

"Go right on in, Mr. Forrest," she said. Then she smiled, and Jake realized that she wasn't being mean, just business-like. "And relax. He's not going to bite you."

Jake had seen a movie once about a private military school for boys. His image of what a headmaster should look like came from that movie. So he half-expected to see a tall, uniformed soldier with a straight back and a stern face staring at him. To his surprise, the man who smiled to him from behind a cluttered desk was small and chubby. He had white hair and a white beard, and he was as round-faced as Santa Claus. "Dr. Cortland Marshall," read the nameplate on his desk. When Dr. Marshall stood up, he was shorter than Jake.

"Sit down, Mr. Forrest," he said.

Jake sat, feeling slightly surprised. Dr. Marshall's voice was at least twice as big as his body, the words coming out in full, round tones. The whole room seemed to reverberate as he spoke.

Dr. Marshall chuckled, clearly aware of the effect his voice had. When he spoke again, his voice was softer, much closer to normal, though still full and deep. He remained standing.

"I've invited you in here this morning for no particular reason, Mr. Forrest. I just wanted to let you know my door is always open. It's a Weltimore tradition that any student may ask to see me whenever he has a real need. Since you were a late admit—although a welcome one—you missed our opening orientation sessions."

Dr. Marshall held up a folder with Jake's name on it. "The teachers at your former school gave you some high praise, young man. Intelligent, cooperative, never a discipline problem, always on time to class. Admirable. Although they do feel you have been hiding your academic light under a bushel. Well, here at Weltimore we are known for bringing out that light in students and helping them make it shine."

Dr. Marshall paused and smiled again at Jake as if he expected Jake to say something.

"Unh-hunh," Jake said, making it an enthusiastic one.

Dr. Marshall's smile broadened, and he patted his desk with both hands as he continued to look down on Jake from his standing position. Jake began to realize just how short the chairs were in Dr. Marshall's office. With the exception of the headmaster's own chair, the other chairs were all so low that anyone sitting on them was practically sitting on the ground. Jake guessed it was one way for Dr. Marshall to make sure people were always looking up at him.

"I know," Dr. Marshall said, "that you may be worrying about how things here are different from your old school. But Weltimore has a long tradition of helping its students from different backgrounds adjust. We have boys here from more than twenty different nations."

Other Indian tribes? Jake found himself thinking. Then he noticed that Dr. Marshall had accompanied his words with an expansive gesture toward a school photo on the wall just five feet from Jake's head. Jake studied the picture for a few minutes, sensing that was what Dr. Marshall expected him to do. A dozen faces of different colors were sprinkled here and there in the photo, smiling young men who mostly looked to be white. Gradually Jake realized that Dr. Marshall meant that there were people from different countries at the school. But he didn't see anyone who looked like an Indian.

Dr. Marshall leaned forward and his voice became more confidential. "I do have one question, Mr. Forrest."

He began to say "unh-hunh," then thought better of it.

"Yes, sir?" he answered.

"How many goals have you been averaging per game this past year?" Dr. Marshall asked, almost in a whisper.

Waiting for Jake's answer, Dr. Marshall leaned closer, so close that Jake noticed for the first time that there were tiny designs on the headmaster's tie. Pictures of tiny people playing lacrosse.

CHAPTER SIX

THE CABINET

BEFORE JAKE REACHED THE DOOR to the guidance office, he stopped to look into the case on the wall. What he had seen from a distance earlier was a lacrosse stick, all right. It was one of the old ones from his great-grandfather's playing days. Jake knew it had to have been handmade, probably by an Indian at Akwesasne, like Frank or Alex Roundpoint. They'd crafted the best Indian sticks back in the 1930s and 1940s.

This stick was in perfect shape. It had been restrung and varnished so that the beautifully shaped hickory wood shone. When Jake looked close enough, though, he could see the scratches and nicks that were a sign of its long use. Jake remembered Grampa Sky telling him what it was like back in the days before plastic sticks. Back then, you'd get shipped a big bundle of sticks, every single one different. Everybody would be excited, first picking up one stick, then another, each one trying to find the stick that fit him just right. Jake wondered whose hands had held this stick, and he wished it wasn't locked up in a glass cabinet.

The old lacrosse stick, though, was only one of the things in the display case. Jake read the large letters above the display: WELTIMORE WARRIORS' PROUD HISTORY. The sign was dominated by a bronze statue of a nearly naked Indian. Jake stared at the mean expression on his face, the two feathers on his head, and the lacrosse stick in his hands. Jake looked back over his shoulder. The thought of anyone seeing him staring at that statue made him feel embarrassed.

It was the way so many people wanted to see Indians—not as real human beings, but as symbols of something fierce and untamed. Jake thought of how Uncle Irwin sometimes joked that more people probably would hire him if he put an Indian like that on his trucks and changed the name of his business from PRINTUP CONTRACTING to NOBLE SAVAGE ROOFING.

Jake knew he should stop staring at the display case,

but his eye was caught by something else now. It was a sort of timeline, a history of lacrosse, "The Fastest Game on Two Feet." It listed such notable dates as 1867, when the Dominion of Canada was formed and lacrosse was proclaimed as its national sport, and 1932 when a lacrosse team from Johns Hopkins University won a gold medal at the Olympic Games in Los Angeles. But it was the first entry that kept Jake's attention most of all:

Lacrosse was played in its most primitive form
by American Indians as a means of training
their young men for war.

Jake shook his head. He wondered how people could love this game so much and know so little about what it meant to the Iroquois people. And what it still means today.

He looked back down the hall toward the front door. Jake wanted to run out that door and keep running until he was back home on the rez where people understood things—understood *him.*

Then he shook his head again. His mother was counting on him to do well in this school. But things were getting really complicated, especially since the headmaster seemed to suggest that he might be their new star attack man. He even mentioned that it would be good if Jake could help the school win the local junior league championship in the spring. What could he do?

Lacrosse, it seemed, was the most important sport at Weltimore Academy. Ever since 1959, when Little League lacrosse was established in the Baltimore area, Weltimore had been the home of the very best junior league teams. Many of the top players on the area prep school teams had been Weltimore stars first. Scorers. Most of them had gone on to colleges like Johns Hopkins, often with full rides on lacrosse scholarships.

"You have come to the right school, my boy," Dr. Marshall had concluded when he ushered Jake out the door.

Now Jake's head was aching. *Why do things have to be so complicated?*

He stopped for a long, cool drink at the drinking fountain. As the water trickled down over his cheek and into the basin, Jake remembered one of the stories Grampa Sky had told him last winter. In that story, a boy lived with his little old grandmother in a little lodge deep in the forest. The only game he played was lacrosse, and he practiced it by himself all the time, throwing the ball and catching it and running as fast as he could. He was so fast that he could even outrun the deer. So his grandmother gave him the name Deer Foot.

When he was twelve-winters-old, Deer Foot decided to search for his lost parents. His little old grandmother told him that monsters out there would try to eat him, but Deer Foot was determined. With his lacrosse stick slung over his shoulder, he set out on the path to the north. As soon as he left the forest, he came to a village by a lake. The people in that lake village greeted him and asked him to come and play a game of lacrosse with him. When he agreed, those people smiled, and Deer Foot saw that they were not really human beings, but terrible creatures. Their lacrosse sticks were made of bones, and their lacrosse ball was a human head.

"When you lose this game," they told Deer Foot, laughing and growling as they spoke, "we will use your head for our new ball."

Jake shook his head. Why had he remembered *that* story? Jake recalled how sad he had been feeling the day Grampa Sky told him that tale. It was one of those times when Jake's mom was supposed to come back and spend time with him, but her schedule had changed, so she hadn't made it.

The story had helped. Even though Deer Foot was outnumbered, he won the lacrosse game against the monsters, who were so frustrated that they threw themselves in the lake and drowned. Then Deer Foot went on to find his parents. The moral of the story: Even in the worst situation, you can find a way out of trouble. After Grampa Sky finished telling the story, Jake had smiled. Now he was frowning again.

Jake wondered what he was going to tell his mom tonight. After all, he had promised her that he wouldn't play lacrosse. Even though he was determined to keep his word, Jake missed the feel of the stick in his hands and the familiar weight of the ball cradled in the webbing as he raced down the field. But he had promised. The headmaster might want him to play lacrosse again, but Jake wouldn't even pick up a stick if his mom really didn't want him to play.

Jake squared his shoulders, turned away from the display case, and went into the guidance office to get his schedule.

❁ ❁ ❁ ❁ ❁

Two adults who had been talking to each other turned to look in Jake's direction as he came in. The bigger of the two men was muscular and had very short blond hair. He was wearing a sweatshirt that read *TERRAPINS*. Jake wasn't sure what "terrapins" meant, but a little design that looked like a turtle was embroidered below the word, so he assumed it must be a turtle of some kind. The shorter man was slender with a long neck. He had thinning, dark-brown hair and glasses, and he wore a suit and tie, like Dr. Marshall. His red, white, and blue tie had stars and stripes on it. No tiny lacrosse players. Jake felt relieved.

Both men grinned at Jake. Why did every adult at this school have to show his teeth at him? Indians didn't grin like that when they met someone for the first time. Jake almost chuckled when he suddenly remembered some-thing he had seen on the Discovery Channel. The show was about baboons, gorillas, and chimpanzees. "Whenever the great apes flash their teeth at each other in a threat-ening grin like this," the narrator said, "it is their way of saying, 'This is my territory, so watch your step.'"

"Mr. Forrest?" said the shorter man, widening his grin as he spoke and leaning his head forward on that long neck.

"Unh-hunh," Jake said.

Then the bigger man took a long step, almost a lunge, toward Jake.

"Coach Walter Scott," he said in a rough voice that was almost a growl. "I'm pleased to meet you, Mr. Forrest." He grabbed Jake's hand in one of those hard, white man handshakes that hurt your fingers. Jake didn't grip back hard, though. Uncle Irwin had told him that most white people shake hands differently than the Indian way. In an Indian handshake, a person just relaxes his hand into the light grasp of the other's. White people might turn a friendly giving of hands into a way of proving one's strength, but Jake wasn't going to do that.

Coach Scott let go of Jake's hand, clearly surprised by the tall boy's limp grasp. But he recovered his composure and put his hand on Jake's left shoulder.

"Well, gentlemen," he rasped, "I have to get to class. I'm your history master. I'll see you there, Mr. Forrest—and on the field." He patted Jake's shoulder once more, and then thrust himself out the door. As soon as he was gone, the whole room seemed to get three times bigger.

Jake turned back toward the thin man who had first greeted him. The man was no longer grinning now that Coach Scott had left the room, but it seemed to Jake that he looked happier.

"Culet," he said, his diction crisp as a leaf of lettuce. "Simpson Culet." He handed a piece of paper to Jake. "Your schedule. Two of our upperclassmen will show you where. Orientation tour. Happy to do that. Chance to skip their first class of the day." Simpson Culet pressed a button on the phone on his desk.

"Yes?" said a voice that sounded like the red-haired woman's.

"Tavares and Kilgore," Mr. Culet said.

"On their way."

A few minutes later, Jake walked along slightly behind the two older boys.

"You'll like it here at Weltimore," Darris Tavares said, pushing open the door to the science room.

"Not," John Kilgore added.

They were almost at the end of their tour, and Jake

still hadn't said more than "hello" and the occasional "unh-hunh" to the two boys. It hadn't bothered them. In fact they hardly seemed to notice. Darris Tavares, who was short, dark-haired, and built like a muscular barrel, had been talking enough for all three of them. John was almost as tall as Jake and was as fair-haired as Darris was dark.

"This is the school computer room. It has all the latest equipment," Darris said.

"Right up to 1986," John Kilgore added.

It had been like that all during the tour. Each time Darris said something, John added a few words that either contradicted Darris or made an ironic comment about whatever he had said. But Jake could tell that the two of them were actually in complete agreement. They were friends the way people are friends when they live together, play together, and respect each other.

Different as they were, John and Darris were alike in one way. They both had pulled the long end of their neckties out of their blazers and had draped them over their left shoulders. It wasn't accidental. Whenever the long end of either boy's tie started to slip down, he would flip it back into place. As they had walked the halls, peering into classes in session, Jake had noticed at least three other boys with their ties over their left shoulders.

The three young men stood in front of a wide, double doorway. Darris put his hand on the handle of one of the doors without opening it. "Our gym," he said.

John smiled for the first time as he put his left hand on the other door handle. "Our gym," he said, reaching up with his right hand to tap the long end of the tie draped over his shoulder.

"We can go in here any time we have a free period, including study halls," Darris said

"Scorer's right," John added.

Then the two of them, together, pushed the handles.

CHAPTER SEVEN

HER DECISION

MOLLY FORREST ADJUSTED her left earring as she watched Jake fill their plates from the cartons of Chinese take-out. Jake was surprised that his mother had said hardly anything. She arrived home with dinner half an hour ago—only an hour later than she'd originally said. Usually she was full of news about her day, about the work they'd done in her office on the battle with the government over the Indian Trust Funds. Today, though, she was so quiet it seemed as if something was wrong.

Jake thought he should ask her if she was okay, but he couldn't stop talking about his day. He'd never felt the need to talk so much. He had so much to say.

"You should see it, Mom," he said. "The whole inside wall of their gym is like this big mural of a college lacrosse game. And they've got the names of all the students who went on and played college lacrosse in this Roll of Honor next to it."

"How are your teachers?" his mother asked.

"Great. I mean, the first thing you see when you go into the school is this display case with what they call a history of lacrosse in it. Although it pretty much leaves out Indians. But it's like the whole school worships lacrosse."

Jake took a deep breath. "They've got this tradition in the school that these two guys who were showing me around, John and Darris, they were telling me about. Like whenever they have a game, the lacrosse players carry their sticks around with them that whole day, wherever they go, into class and everything. And every lacrosse player who has ever scored a goal wears his school tie flopped back over his shoulder."

"You like the other students?"

"They seem pretty cool, Mom," Jake answered. "They were really nice to me—even after I told them I wouldn't be able to play lacrosse."

Molly Forrest took a deep breath, tugged one more time at her earring, and then placed both of her hands palm-down on the table between them. She still hadn't touched the moo goo gai pan Jake had spooned out onto her plate.

"Your headmaster called me today," she said.

Jake's heart thumped in his chest. "Did I do something wrong?" he asked.

Jake's mom shook her head. "No, Jake, but I found myself wondering if *I'd* done something wrong. You know, I never had a chance to visit Weltimore myself. I was just told that it was the best school around here. I didn't know lacrosse was so important to them."

Jake held his breath. Was his mother going to tell him that he couldn't go to Weltimore? Part of him hoped that she would, that she'd tell him it wasn't going to work out for him like she'd thought—the part of him that hoped she'd say he had to go back home to his uncle and aunt and the nation school.

She shook her head again. "And here I thought it was the people I knew who convinced Weltimore to let you in after the usual admission deadline. It seems, though, that your headmaster made some calls to the Nation School as soon as your name came up, just on the chance you might be "one of those Indian boys" who played lacrosse. When he found out how good you were, that tipped the balance."

Jake waited. A different part of him, a part that surprised him, actually wanted to go to Weltimore, to see what it was like there.

Sure, at first he'd felt like he just wanted to run away from a place where they thought Indian lacrosse was primitive and his people were just dumb savages. But as the day had gone on and he'd seen how nice everyone was, how sincere they were, how much they cared about the game, he had found himself thinking differently. A small, stubborn voice in him had grown stronger and stronger. Maybe he could get them to learn more about lacrosse, the true stuff, about what the game really meant to his people. It was the same kind of voice that had kept his mother from giving up when she was the only Indian woman in her law school classes.

Jake's mother sighed. "Jake," she said, "this has been a crazy day for me. Washington seems to get crazier every day, too. Everyone is so tense. First it was airplane crashes and anthrax. Then people were afraid of getting shot by snipers. I don't know where to start. Do you think you can learn to like it here? Do you like this school? Do you think it could work out for you?"

"Unh-hunh," Jake said, hesitantly, unsure of where his mother's thoughts were going.

Molly Forrest reached over to lay her hand on her son's arm. "Well, after talking with your headmaster, I realized I'd made a mistake. I made a mistake by asking you not to play lacrosse. So I'm releasing you from your promise. Jake, you can play lacrosse if you can keep up with your studies and do well in every class. Understand? Every class."

"Unh-hunh," Jake said, an "unh-hunh" that let her know that he agreed, but also that he knew she still had said only part of what she wanted to say.

"In a way," Jake's mom continued, "it was good that Dr. Marshall called when he did." Her voice turned more serious.

Whatever it is, Jake thought, *here it comes.*

"Jake, I've also realized that this just isn't working out the way I thought it would, with my crazy schedule. You've been left alone here far too much. And you shouldn't have to come home to an empty house all the time. As nice as this condo is for me, it hasn't been much fun for you, has it?"

Jake didn't answer, but his mom nodded.

"Just as I thought. Today they told me that I was going to be doing even more on this case. I'm going to be making a bigger salary, but I also have to do more travel and even be away on weekends. Well, as soon as I heard that, I knew I had to make a big decision."

I'm going home, Jake thought, trying not to smile. He could already see the welcoming look on Uncle Irwin's face, could even smell Aunt Alice's cooking.

"So," Jake's mom said, patting his arm, "I worked it out over the phone with Dr. Marshall. They have the space in their dorm for you. You're going to be a boarding student at Weltimore."

CHAPTER EIGHT
DRILLS

"SCOOP THE BALL, MR. KURESHI," Coach Scott growled. "This isn't golf."

Muhammad Kuyreshi, a Pakistani boy who was one of Jake's two new roommates, took another quick running step and managed to thrust the head of his lacrosse stick under the elusive ball. He cradled it uncertainly, and then threw it. It bounced weakly over the ground, then rolled toward the next player in the opposite line, about twenty yards away.

As Muhammad turned and ran back to the end of their line, he gave a quick thumbs-up to Jake, who nodded to him. Before lights-out last night, Jake had showed Muhammad the right technique for scooping. He had played field hockey back home, but never lacrosse.

Sweat ran down Jake's face, but he didn't wipe it away. He was next in line and had to concentrate. The players had been on the field doing defensive drills for at least half an hour. Shuttle run. Foot fire. Fast break. Triangle slide. Defensive clearing. Jake was in the familiar place his mind and body went to during practices and games. Nothing else existed except this moment. He was aware only of the stick in his hand, the ball, the other players, the field, and the commands of his coach.

The ball rocketed toward him, fired hard by John Kilgore's long arms, across the hard surface of the field. Jake gathered it in the webbing of his stick, cradled up, spun, and rolled back across. This stick wasn't like his old one, still back at the res. But he'd gotten used to this plastic stick, and it moved in his hands as if it were part of him. Of course, Jake wasn't aware of how he looked on the field, but the other players were. His moves were as smooth and flowing as a bird's wing cutting through the air.

An hour later, the practice over, Jake sat on a bench in the boys' locker room. He was alone, and everything that had not intruded on his mind while he was on the field came flooding back. He had already taken his shower and dressed. He had to get to dinner soon, but here he sat, trying to understand how he felt.

A month had passed since his arrival at Weltimore, and he'd been a boarding student for three weeks. His two roommates, Muhammad Kureshi and Kofi Anloga, were good guys. He'd never spent time with anyone from another country before, and it was kind of cool. It was interesting to hear about their homes and their families in Pakistan and Ghana. Somehow, as far away as their homes were, Jake felt as if his own home was even further. Crazy. He knew it was only an eight-hour bus ride to the reservation.

"Hey," a voice said. "Earth to Jake."

Jake looked up. Darris Tavares stood there, his earphones on. Electronic equipment wasn't allowed in class, but after 5:00 P.M., everyone broke out his stuff. The sound was cranked so loud Jake could hear Pearl Jam streaming out. Darris liked the old stuff. He turned down the volume on his player, which was half the size and ten times as expensive as the old Walkman Jake was holding. Jake had noticed that everything personal that the kids at this school owned, whether it was a sweater or a picture frame, was top-of-the-line, stuff Jake had only seen in mall windows or on TV ads.

"Coming to dinner?" Darris asked him. "Come on."

Jake stood up and looked over Darris's shoulder. John Kilgore was standing in the doorway, waiting for both of them. That was how it was around here. The guys were always trying to make him feel at home, letting him know he was included. Even when they had short-sheeted his bed the first night in the dorm and put shaving cream into his sneakers, Jake knew it was something every kid had to go through, like a ritual. Everybody had laughed about it, and he had smiled along with them. Everything they did made him feel included.

After he'd started practicing with the team, they'd been even more friendly. They taught him to accept the privileges given to the lacrosse kids—like wearing his tie over his shoulder or being allowed to go into the gym whenever he had a free period, so he could use the weight machines or just shoot baskets. He was as much a part of this special group at Weltimore as any of the others. So why did Jake feel even more like a stranger?

Maybe it was because he felt it was just part of the drill. Maybe they were doing it because they were supposed to do it. Or was it just because he was a new player on a team, someone who would make them more likely to be winners because he was part of the team? He often wondered if they would even talk to him if he didn't play lacrosse.

"Ready?" Darris asked.

In the doorway, John waved at him. "Let's go."

"Unh-hunh," Jake said. He stood up and followed them.

🏯 🏯 🏯 🏯 🏯

Jake actually looked forward to most of his classes. He had discovered that if he really concentrated on what was being taught, he could forget everything else in his life for those few moments—until the bell sounded to move them on to the next room. It was nothing like the Nation School. He didn't have his best buddy Rick Jamieson passing him notes or Frank Tarbell making signs at him from the other side of the room, reminding him they were riding their bikes up around Frogtown that afternoon, fun things that kept him from focusing on his schoolwork.

The teachers at Weltimore weren't really that much better; he just paid better attention here. By concentrating on his school subjects, Jake didn't leave himself any room to think about how much he missed his aunt and uncle and his friends back home.

When he was in class, Jake didn't have to think about being part of a new team. He didn't have time to wonder why he sometimes felt so uncomfortable about being one of "Coach Scott's Boys." In class, all he had to do was be a math student or a science student or an English student. As a result, he was doing better than he had ever done before, getting a low A in everything. In his biology class, Jake was paired up as lab partner with Skippy Fairbanks, the smartest of the "Smart Kids."

History, though, was a little different. Coach Scott was the history master. Sometimes Coach Scott ran the class like any other class, and Jake could make his mental escape, safe in the middle of facts and dates, names and places. But whenever Coach Scott brought lacrosse into the history lesson, Jake didn't feel more at home. Instead, it always made him feel uneasy.

"War is like being out on the playing field," Coach Scott would growl. "In both cases, winning is not the most important thing." Then he would pause and look around the room.

Jake was careful always to have his gaze down, looking at his desk, focusing on the end of his pen as he took notes when Coach Scott did that. In those long pauses, Coach Scott would stare at one boy after another, as if daring one of them to speak up and challenge what he was saying. No one ever did. Then, like a player raising his hands after scoring a goal, he'd make his point.

"No, winning is not the most important thing. It's the ONLY thing!"

History was the only class that made Jake think about home. It was the only class that made him remember, regardless of how hard everyone had tried to make him fit in, that he was different.

Although everyone at Weltimore wore the same school uniform, it somehow made the differences between them even more obvious. It wasn't the clothes the other boys wore—it was the way they wore them, things like a Scorer draping his necktie over his shoulder. Jake kept forgetting to do that. More than once, one of the kids on his team had come up to him in the hall and reached out, almost as automatically as giving a high-five, to lift Jake's tie up for him and put it back over his shoulder.

People's faces were more distinct because of the uniform, too. Faces like Muhammad's or Kofi's or Jake's stood out, clearly different from the others'. Sometimes Jake could see in the faces of the Third Generation students, the "Three-Gens," those whose fathers and grandfathers had gone to Weltimore, a look that told him what they were thinking.

Uncle Irwin had always told Jake that he should never think that making a lot of money was the goal of life. Jake knew that the Three-Gen boys had been told just the opposite. Sometimes, when Jake saw them looking at him, he was sure they were thinking about how much more they had than this poor Indian kid.

In the locker room, for example, the Three-Gens sometimes talked about what kind of cars their fathers were going to buy for them when they turned sixteen. None of them was going to get a Ford or a Chevy. Jake could only shake his head when he heard the names "Porsche" or "Benz." It was just that way for those kids— part of their family history.

Jake remembered a point the coach had made once about history. "Studying history," Coach Scott had said, "is just like getting a chance to play the same team twice in the season. What you learn the first time around will help you avoid the mistakes of the past." Jake had a feeling that most of the other kids just wanted to keep repeating the same rich history. They wanted to do what their fathers had done, to have what their parents had.

But then again, so did he. But what he wanted was way different, especially the way he looked at history itself.

Jake remembered Grampa Sky saying just that. "We don't see the same history the white people see. Our history is not dead facts in a book. Our history is alive and still going on. It's in our songs and stories and in the roots of every tree."

Still, Jake forced himself to pay attention to what Coach Scott said. If a student was caught daydreaming, the coach made him go stand at attention at the front of the room. Muhammad Kureshi was already in front of the chalkboard, his back stiff as a ramrod.

"Tomorrow," Coach Scott boomed, "we're going to take a little detour into an event in 1763, a little story I know you'll enjoy."

The bell rang, but Jake didn't move. Neither did

anyone else. The class knew Coach Scott's drill.

Coach Scott looked around the room, smiled, and then bellowed, "Dis-missed!"

CHAPTER NINE
ANOTHER DAY

JAKE LOOKED OUT THE DORM WINDOW. The sun was just starting to show itself above the trees. He held up the glass of water in his hands, waiting for the first light of dawn to pass through it.

"Elder Brother," Jake whispered, "I thank you for giving us another day."

Then Jake drank the water. He did this every morning. No one else was awake yet, so no one was around to ask him what he was doing. Grampa Sky had taught him this was a good thing to do. It would remind Jake to be thankful every day for the many blessings, great and small, that most people take for granted.

"When the light of the Old One, the Great Sun, touches water," Grampa Sky had told him, "that water becomes a medicine. Drink it and it will keep you strong, grandson."

Jake heard a cough from behind him. He turned around quickly and looked toward Kofi's bed against the western wall of the dorm room. He caught Kofi, halfway between watching and pulling the sheet back over his head. Found out, Kofi propped himself up on one arm and smiled at Jake.

"So, you have caught me observing your morning ceremonies," Kofi said in his half-British accent. The lilt and rhythm of Kofi's voice, his precise use of language, always made Jake think his West African roommate was about to break into song.

"Unh-hunh," Jake said slowly, meaning he knew Kofi had something more to say.

"It takes you home, what you do every morning. Does it not?" Kofi asked.

Jake nodded.

Kofi's smile broadened. "And just so, I also wait every morning for the light of the new day that comes from the East, from Africa where my family lives, to touch my face, knowing they, too, have smiled up at Mawu, the same great sun that shows the power of God."

Kofi took a small leather pouch from under his

pillow. "My uncle prepared this for me. He is a well educated man with his master's degree and a faithful Methodist, but he was also taught to be a priest in our old religion. This pouch contains things that protect me when I am far from home. Every now and then, when no one else can see, I hold it up so it, too, can bathe in the light of the African sun." Kofi chuckled as he put the pouch back under his pillow. "So, Jake, it seems that we are brothers. We each have secrets we keep from the white eyes."

Jake laughed as he held out his hand and took Kofi's to shake it, ending with the Ghanian finger snap that Kofi had taught him soon after they became roommates.

"Brothers," Jake agreed, turning to look at Muhammad's bed against the northern wall of their room, wondering if he, too, had been watching. But, like every morning, the figure curled under the covers made no motion. Muhammad was always the last one to rise, but he was never late to morning assembly. Jake wondered about that.

"Ah, have you not noticed?" Kofi said, as if he were reading Jake's mind. Kofi hopped out of bed, crossed the room, and pulled back Muhammad's covers. Instead of their shy Pakistani roommate, Jake saw two pillows rolled together to look like a sleeping body. "Every morning, even before you, Muhammad goes quietly from our room. He has a place where he can spread out his rug and offer his morning prayer toward Mecca. Though he has not told you of it, I know he would not mind your knowing. After all, we three have much in common, do we not?"

A while later, Jake and Kofi walked together across the common between their dorm and the assembly hall where each new school day began. Jake thought about how little most people know about each other. It seemed as if most of the kids—and the teachers, too—didn't really want to get to know who you really were. They were just satisfied with knowing the role you played. The Three-Gens, for example, were like royalty at the school. That seemed to be enough for them. Jake might be Indian, but because he was so good at lacrosse, his main identity at Weltimore was that as one of the Scorers. Kofi might be from Ghana, but because he always seemed to have the answer in every class, he was known to everybody as one of the Smart Kids.

Muhammad's identity was that of a kid who was trying to play a new sport and, as a result, didn't know how to do anything right. It was still a struggle for him to figure out how to catch and throw a lacrosse ball. Muhummad's own favorite sport was field hockey, but he no longer mentioned that to anyone.

"In America," one of the Three-Gens told Muhammad, "field hockey is a girls' sport. Do you wear a dress when you play it?"

It was like that in class, too. Muhammad seemed to always be the one who made mistakes—the one who had to stand at attention in Coach Scott's class or had to take home extra assignments in math or was assigned remedial tutoring in science.

Jake shook his head. It was even worse than that for Muhammad. Because of the things that had happened with Middle Eastern terrorists, because of all the panic on the news, some people looked at Jake's Pakistani friend in a very different way, a way that wasn't good. They looked at him with suspicion and uncertainty, as if he might suddenly turn dangerous. Jake knew it was the same way some people about a hundred years ago looked at American Indians.

Muhammad was already in his seat when Jake and Kofi entered the assembly hall, so they sat down next to him. As always, Kofi's tie was perfectly knotted, good enough to be in an ad in *Gentleman's Quarterly*. But Muhammad's rumpled tie looked as if it had started as a four-in-hands, tried halfway through to turn into a bow, and then gave up. He'd get demerits for sure when Coach Scott saw it. Of all the teachers, Coach Scott was the worst about enforcing the dress code.

Kofi reached over and shook Muhammad's hand, smiling when the shake ended with a satisfyingly loud snap of both their fingers. Muhammad laughed out loud. It was the first time he'd gotten the finger snap right. Jake laughed with his two friends. It was another day at school and maybe, just maybe, it would be a better one.

CHAPTER TEN

COACH SCOTT'S STORY

JAKE CLOSED HIS EYES, wishing he could close his ears at the same time. A long thirty minutes remained until the end of the class. Coach Scott had been talking for just a few minutes. He was telling the story he'd promised, the one about that event in 1763. Just as Jake had feared, it was another story with Indians in it, but it was even worse than he had expected. And, of course, it was also about lacrosse.

"As the sun rose higher over Fort Michilimackinac, beside the great lake, not far from present-day Detroit, the poor English soldiers had no idea what they were in for that day," Coach Scott said, building the suspense.

Even with his eyes closed, Jake could imagine the grim smile on Coach Scott's face. Stories like this one, tales that ended up with blood and death, made Coach Scott's classes really popular. Somehow, just about every historical event he described seemed to end up in a pitched battle. Coach Scott loved warrior tales.

"The local Ojibwe were angry at the English, who had just taken over the fort from the French, former allies of those Indians. Those Ojibwes had also heard that the great war chief, Pontiac, was calling for all the tribes to revolt and throw out the English," Coach Scott continued. "But the English soldiers were strong and well-armed. The walls of the fort were high. The only hope the Indian warriors had was treachery. So they announced they were going to have a big lacrosse game, right there in front of the fort."

Jake put his head down onto his arms, folded on top of his desk. He could feel the other students stealing glances in his direction as Coach Scott continued his story. After all, Jake was the only Indian. Jake worried that maybe they were wondering right now if he was just as mean as those "treacherous" Ojibwes.

Coach Scott took a breath, then continued. "The innocent white soldiers left the gate of the fort open while they watched the game. They had no idea what was happening when the lacrosse ball was thrown, as if by accident, through the gate and into the fort. The soldiers laughed as the Ojibwe ballplayers rushed madly into the fort, supposedly in pursuit of the ball. But the white men's laughter stopped when those lacrosse players pulled out hidden weapons and began to massacre the surprised soldiers."

"All right!" somebody said from the back of the class. Jake recognized the voice. Sam Sewall, one of the Three-Gens.

Coach Scott smiled as he paused from telling his story. Jake knew what came next—it was time for one of the coach's funny remarks, usually a bad pun, something that would make the boys in the class laugh.

"So it was," Coach Scott said, "that the old warriors' game was used as a trick to wipe out those English soldiers. That was one lacrosse game that truly ended, you might say, with the thrill of victory and the agony of defeat."

"Game over," Sam Sewall said as almost everyone in the class began to chuckle. Doug Radebaugh, who was sitting to Jake's right didn't laugh. Of all the Three-Gens, Doug was the quietest. Even though he was a terrific goalie, he didn't make a big deal about it. He glanced over at Jake. Jake looked away.

"In fact," Coach Scott added, with a smirk, "that might have been the first 'sudden-death overtime.'"

Just as he expected, the class went wild with laughter.

After class, Jake walked down the hall and turned off into the boys' restroom. It was empty. All the other kids were hurrying to their next class. Jake went back to the furthest stall, one with a lock that still worked, sat down, and latched the door. He leaned over and put his head in his hands. He felt so sad, angry, and confused that he didn't know what to do. He had no doubt that Coach Scott's story was right out of a history book. He'd gone to the library the last time Coach Scott mentioned Indians just to look up what the coach had said. Jake found that the facts in a book agreed with the coach's version. But Jake felt there had to be more to these stories than just what the books reported. He knew there was always more than one side to a story. That was why, Grampa Sky had told him, Sonkwaiatison, the Creator, gave human beings two ears—so we could always listen to both sides.

Jake always asked himself the same questions: Why did Coach Scott always make his stories about Indians so bloody, always tales about war and battles and killing? And why did he have to make lacrosse a part of that? Lacrosse was more than just a game, more than just a way of getting ready for war. Being a real warrior, in the Indian way, didn't mean killing people. It didn't mean setting yourself above others or bullying people and telling them what to be. To be a true warrior meant that no matter how strong or skilled you were, you had to stay humble. You had to work to help others, be ready to defend the people when they needed your help. To be a true warrior meant you had to love peace and keep that love of peace in your heart.

"I wish I could tell him," Jake said to himself in a soft voice. But even as he said it, he felt sure there was no way he could make Coach Scott—or any of them— really listen.

CHAPTER ELEVEN

GAME DAY

I T ALL HAPPENED IN LESS TIME than it took to count to ten. But it was as if everything was moving in slow motion, just as it often seemed when Jake was into the flow of a game. It was like time didn't exist or as if Jake had all the time in the world to work his moves.

"Drop in, Mack, drop in!" the goalie shouted to the defender who was supposed to be on Jake.

Jake smiled as he ran. The goalie had seen what Number 18, the defender in front of Jake, had not. He was playing Jake too far from the goal. Jake lowered his chin and pushed out his lower lip. He stepped right, planted his foot, and spun left. Number 18 stumbled and fell forward.

"Tommy!" the goalie yelled to the one defender left in front of Jake, "Move out! Move out!"

But Tommy, Number 19, was too late to close in on

Jake and screen out the net. Jake passed him like a diving hawk. The goalie stepped back into the crease, holding up his stick, just waiting for Jake's shot. Jake could see that the goalie was sure it would be a high shot, like the one Jake had taken when he scored his second goal.

At the last second, though, Jake brought his lacrosse stick down and dipped for a low sidearm shot, going into a forward roll onto his left shoulder The ball struck the ground, went between the goalie's legs, and slammed into the net. Jake bounced to his feet at the same moment the ref called, "Goal!"

The whistle blew. Jake stood, as he always did after a goal, holding his stick in his right hand, his head down. It was something his uncle had shown him long ago, an old salute to the Sun, the one who gives life and light to all things. The Sun loves to watch lacrosse being played well.

"Thank you, Elder Brother," Jake said softly. Then he dropped his stick down. He never held his pose for long. He didn't do it to call attention to himself. It had just become as natural to him as cradling the ball or shooting. Now he was hardly aware that he gave his thanks that way. But Jake had done it enough times that others on his team knew it and had come to expect it.

From his place on the bench, where he spent every game, Muhammad caught Jake's eye and gave him a thumbs-up. Darris and John, who had each scored a goal, too, ran up to high-five Jake.

"Fifth hat trick in five games," Darris said as he slapped Jake's hand and then hugged him. "Way to go, Super Chief!"

"We're gonna kill the league," John yelled. "Yooooo! Weltimore rules!"

"Okay, men," Coach Scott called from the sidelines. He sounded happy. "Over here, bring it in."

Pushing Jake ahead of them, the two team captains joined the circle around their coach. Coach Scott held out his right hand, palm down. One after another, the Weltimore lacrosse players stacked their right hands on top of his. Tentatively, Jake added his hand. The coach looked around the circle of grinning faces, pausing just for a moment to nod at Jake. "Good game, men," he rasped. "Radebaugh, great job in the net. Now let's hear it!"

"WAH WAH, WELTIMORE!
WARRIORS WIN!
WAH WAH, WELTIMORE!
WIN AGAIN!"

The team walked off the field after shaking hands with their opponents, who had lost 11 to 3. Kofi waved at Jake from the crowd. Jake raised his hand to him and nodded.

Darris, who had kept his arm around Jake's shoulder, leaned in to speak to him.

"Hey, Chief," Darris said.

Jake winced a little. Chief. Super Chief. Somehow he'd gotten those two names. He didn't know when or how, but once you were given a nickname on a school team, it was harder to get rid of than dried gum on the bottom of your sneakers. He'd thought of telling them that he didn't like the names, that being a chief was a sacred thing and that he really wasn't one. But he hadn't been able to get the words out, mainly because he knew they didn't mean to hurt his feelings.

It was crazy, he thought, how so many of things they did to show him they liked him and approved of him instead made him feel so uncomfortable. Instead of making him feel included, they made him feel like more of an outsider. It was as if a glass wall was between him and the other kids on the team, and only he knew it was there.

"Yes?" Jake said.

"We were just wondering why you always do that after a goal. You know, raise your stick up with your head down like that?" Darris asked.

"Yeah," John said. "That some kind of Indian victory thing, like a war dance or something?"

Jake's face felt hot. His mouth seemed to be full of cotton. Somehow, though, he managed to keep the smile on his face and to speak.

"No," Jake said. "It's just a way of saying thanks."

Darris laughed. "Thanks? Man, with the talent you got, you don't gotta say thanks to nobody, Chief."

"No way, José," John added, poking Jake playfully in the chest.

Jake didn't say anything. The smile was still on his face. But the glass wall was getting thicker.

CHAPTER TWELVE
RUNNING HOME

JAKE WASN'T SURE how he was going to get through the school gate. It was almost always locked, open only when the cars and buses came through at the start of school and at the end of the day. Weltimore had two extra security guards in place to ensure the safety of the students and staff. Since the second week Jake had been at Weltimore, security had been dramatically increased. Even though the police had caught the two men who'd been randomly shooting people, the security stayed. Instead of feeling safer, Jake felt more like a prisoner.

But, somehow, today he had to get out. He shifted the backpack over his shoulder and tried to walk as silently as a shadow down the main hall of the classroom building. He wasn't sure why he had decided to do it this way. He could have made it easy for himself and have left the dorm while everyone was at breakfast. Jake didn't even remember eating breakfast, but he knew he must have. He must have gotten dressed and eaten and gone to morning assembly and then to class, because here he was.

His mind was all mixed up, filled with worry and uncertainty about everything—except one thing. He knew he had to get back home. He had just received word about the accident, about Uncle Irwin getting hurt. Jake was told that the doctors weren't sure that his uncle was going to survive. Jake knew he had to get home and see him.

Somehow, Jake thought, *if I can get home to see him, he'll be okay.*

Jake remembered the story Grampa Sky had told him about Jim Thorpe, the Sac and Fox Indian who had been the world's greatest athlete. Jim Thorpe had won the decathlon and pentathlon at the Olympic Games in Sweden in 1912. He'd played both professional baseball and football. Grampa Sky had known him. They hadn't gone to Carlisle Indian School together—Grampa Sky wasn't that old—but when Grampa Sky was a teenage boy, Jim Thorpe had come to their reservation one summer and had watched the young men play lacrosse. That day, even though the famous athlete was fifty-years-old at the time, Jim Thorpe had rolled up his sleeves, taken off his shoes, and borrowed a lacrosse stick so he could play with them.

"And he was a good lacrosse player," Grampa Sky said. "Scored five goals in ten minutes!"

At the end of the game, Jim Thorpe sat down and talked with Grampa Sky. Somehow he had heard that Grampa Sky was a Carlisle boy and that he was thinking about not going back for his last year at Carlisle. Just like Jake, Grampa Sky wanted to stay home. So Jim Thorpe told Grampa Sky a story. He told about how when he was first at an Indian boarding school, Haskell Institute, not Carlisle, he got word that his father had been shot in a hunting accident.

"Even though my home in Oklahoma was hundreds of miles away from Haskell, way up there in Kansas," Jim Thorpe said, resting his arm around Grampa Sky's shoulder, "I just took off running. I didn't pack no bag or look back. I just knew I had to get home." Then Jim Thorpe laughed. "I was in such a hurry to get home that

I ran a hundred miles in the wrong direction to start with. It took me two weeks to get home, and when I got there, my father was waiting for me, all recovered from that accident."

Grampa Sky had waited to see what Jim Thorpe would say next, thinking maybe he would tell him that school was important, that he had to go back for that last year no matter what. But Jim Thorpe just sat there for a long time, looking out over the lacrosse field. Then he squeezed Grampa Sky's shoulder, got up, and walked over to put on his shoes, get into his car, and drive away.

"I decided," Grampa Sky said, "that the lesson his story was supposed to teach me was to always make sure I knew where I was going before I started to run. So I went back and finished my last year at Carlisle before I came home for good."

I won't run the wrong way, Jake thought.

He looked down the hall. Thomas Jones, the security guard who had met Jake during his first day of school, sat at his desk right around the corner. Jake said hello to him every day. Jake always said hello to every adult he saw each day, even the grounds people, whom most of the other kids ignored as if they were invisible. Thomas always nodded and smiled at him, but Jake knew Thomas wouldn't let him out of the building while classes were in session.

Jake turned down another hall, one he hadn't noticed before. He was glad to see that it led to the back of the building. There was a back door that read *EXIT*.

Jake pushed open the back door. All he saw was a little lawn, a few trees, and the wall. No one would see him except a fox squirrel digging by the base of a sycamore. Jake ran toward the wall. Maybe, if he could just reach it before anyone saw him, he could get over the wall.

No one saw him. When he got there, he was surprised to see how easy the wall was to climb. The bricks stuck out like tiny steps, and he was up the wall and over it in no time. He knew he had to find the bus station in town. He looked old enough to travel by himself, and if he just acted confident, he figured he could buy a ticket without much notice.

Jake counted his money again, less than he had remembered having. The last time he'd counted it, there had been almost a hundred dollars. Now, for some reason, he had only twenty-eight dollars. Twenty-eight dollars. Jake remembered Coach Scott saying that was how much the Dutch paid in trading goods for Manhattan Island when they bought it from the "dumb Indians." Twenty-eight dollars. Jake shook his head at the irony, wondering, *Is the asking price for Manhattan enough to buy one Indian kid's way home?*

Jake began to run along the road. He ran for a long, long time, heading for town, for the bus station. He felt as if he could run forever as long as he was heading home. But he knew he didn't have two weeks like Jim Thorpe did. He hoped he was heading the right way.

A car pulled up next to him.

"Hey," a friendly voice said, "where you going?"

Jake was afraid it was a policeman, someone sent to get him. He got ready to turn and run away from the road. But then he realized the words that had been spoken to him weren't in English. They'd been in Iroquois! Jake looked at the car.

An old woman was leaning out the passenger side. Jake didn't know her, but he could see she was Indian. Her face was so kind that he trusted her right away.

"Grandmother," Jake answered in Iroquois, "I am

trying to get home. My beloved uncle is hurt."

"Ah, grandson," the old woman said. "We are going there now. Climb in. We will take you."

The next thing Jake knew, he was in the car. He leaned back and closed his eyes. He suddenly realized how tired he was from his running.

"We will be there in no time at all, grandson," the old woman said.

And Jake knew that they would. He would open his eyes and they would be on the winding road that led past the lacrosse field. They would be pulling into Uncle Irwin's driveway, and he and Aunt Mary would be waiting. Uncle Irwin would be well and strong, and their dog Bear would be standing with them, barking with joy when he saw Jake. Jake could hear him now. He opened his eyes to look out the car window.

But when Jake opened his eyes, the car window was gone. He turned his head on his pillow and saw the picture of his uncle and aunt and Bear on the table by his bed. It was just where it had been when he had gone to sleep the night before. And he was just where he had been.

I'm still at Weltimore.

For a moment, Jake thought he was going to cry. It had been a dream. He had not run away and gone home.

Then he realized that if it was just a dream, then Uncle Irwin was not hurt. Jake felt the fear drain from his body. It *was* a dream. But Jake knew that it was more than that. A dream like that didn't just come for no reason. Aunt Alice and Uncle Irwin and Grampa Sky, all the Indian people he knew and trusted most, had told him to listen to his dreams. A dream could be a message from the Creator. A dream could help you and give you strength.

Jake had no idea what message his dream carried, but he felt a warmth surround him. He remembered how gentle and sweet that old woman's voice in his dream had been. It made him feel for a moment as if he actually had been home with those he loved.

"*Niaweh*, Grandmother," Jake said. "Thank you."

CHAPTER THIRTEEN
SHOT

EVEN BEFORE JAKE AND HIS ROOMMATES reached the assembly hall that morning, they knew something was wrong. The security guards were standing at attention by the closed school gate. A police cruiser was parked at the front of the administration building. Jake heard the tiny, insect-like voices from two-way radios cut through the morning quiet of the campus.

As the other kids moved from the dorms toward the assembly hall, Jake noticed that everyone was quieter than usual. Any talking going on was in whispers. Some students were looking over their shoulders, trying to keep close to the big sycamores that lined the walkway, darting from tree to tree like soldiers entering a town that might be occupied by the enemy.

Jake knew what everyone was thinking. They were

fearful that the police car and the high security meant there might be another sniper loose—some new faceless menace out there, angry at the world.

"What good is whispering going to do?" Kofi said to Jake. "Soft voice does not protect man from a bullet. My uncle was a soldier for the West African defense force in Sierra Leone, and he always said that."

"Unh-hunh," Jake said. He couldn't think of any other answer.

Muhammad shook his head. "I am sorry for your countrymen, Jake," he said. "There are too many people now who just want to hurt others."

Doug Radebaugh came running down the steps of the assembly hall toward them. Doug was more than a Three-Gen; he was one of those students they called a "Legacy," a Maryland kid whose family had been coming to the school ever since it was founded. But Doug never acted as if that made him a celebrity. Jake liked Doug the best of all his teammates. He was almost as quiet as Jake and had never called Jake "Chief" or made any remark about Indians. An uncle of Doug's had played on a Terrapins squad that had two Native Americans on it.

Like his all-American uncle, Doug was a genius as a goalie and just about always stopped every shot.

"Jake," Doug whispered. "Did you hear what happened?"

Jake shook his head.

"Oh man," Doug said, his voice getting louder. "It's awful. Coach Scott just got shot this morning. They say he's dead."

CHAPTER FOURTEEN
SECURE

THE FIRST FEW HOURS OF THAT DAY passed Jake like shapes moving in a thick fog. He would see a face when one of the shapes drew close enough, and then it would vanish again into the haze, leaving him alone with his confused thoughts.

How could anyone do something evil like this? It was almost too much for Jake to grasp. An attack from an enemy was something that his people understood. In the old days, they had known who the enemy was. Even when his people fought the white men, those wars had had rules. But now it was as if there were no rules about anything. How could people live if the enemies were invisible? If they shot people for no reason at all? How can people deal with a world like that?

No one seemed to know what to do or say, even the adults in charge of the school. Jake sensed that they were trying their best, trying not to scare people. But when Dr. Marshall got up to the podium and said, "There's nothing to worry about—the campus has been locked down and secured," it didn't make anyone feel safer.

Because rumors were already flying, Dr. Marshall explained that he wanted to tell them everything he knew about what had happened. He said it was true that a member of the faculty had been injured, and that as soon as he was able to say more, he would let everyone know.

"For now," he ended, "everyone should proceed to his first class. In the interest of safety, all the blinds will be drawn in every room. This will make the building more secure."

Secure? Jake felt just the opposite. The whispering around him grew louder. Rumors flew through the school like a flock of wild birds frightened into flight by a hunter. Jake heard that Coach Scott had been shot through the head, that he was on life support, that the hospital was already donating his organs.

Jake tried not to listen, tried to think of something else. How could Coach Scott be hurt? He was granite, as hard and invulnerable as stone. Jake thought about how he had been feeling toward the coach, how angry he had felt about some of the things Coach Scott had said in class. Jake thought of how frustrated he had felt in practice at times, like when Coach Scott praised him for his "killer instinct." Just last week Jake had almost walked out of a pregame huddle when Coach Scott ended his pep talk with the words, "Now let's go get some scalps." The anger he remembered feeling toward his coach made Jake feel strange now that the man had been hurt—or maybe even killed. A part of Jake felt responsible. He felt guilty.

After a long morning, the students were called in for a special assembly at noon.

"I have news about Coach Scott," the headmaster said. He paused and looked out over the audience. "He's alive."

A murmur that almost turned into a cheer went through the crowd. But Dr. Marshall raised one hand, knocking on the podium with the other to call for quiet.

"First I have to dispel some rumors. I know that faculty and students alike have been talking about what happened. I now have a report from the police. What happened was an accident of sorts. On his way to work this morning, Coach Scott stopped for coffee at a convenience store. A man with a handgun came in to rob the store. When the clerk resisted, the man began shooting wildly. Our Coach Scott moved to shield a woman who was holding a small child. Coach Scott kept them from being hurt, but he was shot and was gravely wounded as a result."

Dr. Marshall looked out over the sea of faces that stared up at him, faces of boys who were relieved that their coach and teacher was alive, that he had not been a victim of yet another faceless sniper. Still, the boys were shocked about what had happened and were moved by their coach's courage.

"We're being kept informed about his condition by Coach's family. When we know more, we'll tell you. Please keep Coach Scott and his family in your thoughts today, boys."

❀   ❀   ❀   ❀   ❀

Jake slowly opened his eyes and then sat up. He was in his room. He was not on a green lacrosse field near a wide, flowing river. There were no cornfields growing along the field's edge, no bark-covered longhouses on the hill above the fields. Although Jake knew he was in his room at Weltimore, a part of him was still on that field.

It was not only that this dream had been more real than any of the others he'd had recently. It was also that the dream was still with him, still within him. He could still hear an old man's voice speaking to him, a voice he had never heard before, yet seemed as familiar to him as the voice of his own grandfather.

He looked at the calendar on the wall near his bed. Barely enough light allowed him to make out the numbers on it. Since coming to Weltimore, he had marked off each day before going to sleep, knowing he was that many days closer to being able to go home. But for the last three days, since Coach Scott was shot, he hadn't bothered to cross off the days.

What had happened to the coach made his own homesickness seem small and petty. Jake still felt guilty, that it was somehow his fault, all because he had felt so angry at Coach Scott. Jake realized that he'd been wrong about Coach in at least one way. True, the coach had been insensitive in saying the things he said about Indians, but he also had tried to protect someone, and had gotten hurt doing so. Jake nodded to himself as he realized that Coach Scott had reacted like a real warrior, one who risks himself for the people.

I have to do something, Jake thought. And, just like that, he felt the power of his dream, and an idea came to him. At first he tried to push the idea away.

There's no way I can even tell anyone my idea. No one will understand. They'll just think I'm weird. They'll either laugh or they won't listen.

Jake looked at his lacrosse stick leaning in the corner of the room. If he told people about his idea, he could lose it all. He could lose the respect he'd gained in the eyes of his teammates. Even worse, what if they didn't respect what he wanted to share with them? Jake tried to dismiss the idea, but like a little bird tapping on a window, it wouldn't go away.

He thought about what his mom had said to him over the phone two nights ago. He'd been surprised to get her call because it wasn't her usual weekly phone day, and he knew she'd been out of the country. It had been quite an honor for her to be chosen to go to this conference in Geneva, Switzerland. She'd told him she doubted there would be time for her to call him. But she had.

"Are you all right?" were her first words.

"Unh-hunh," Jake answered, still half-asleep. Her call had come after he had gone to bed. The dorm advisor had come to his room to get him and take him down to the phone room. No personal phones were allowed on campus, so all calls went through the office.

"Honey," she had said, "do you want to go home?"

"What?" Those were the last words Jake had expected to hear. A while ago, they would have made his heart leap in his chest. But now they just confused him.

"I'm sorry, this satellite connection must be bad. I asked if you wanted to go home. I heard the news about what happened to your coach, Jake. It made me wonder if I had done the right thing, not only by putting you in that school, but taking you away from the only real home you've ever known. I just . . . I don't know . . . Jake?"

Her voice trailed away. Jake could imagine her tugging at her earring. She sounded so uncertain—almost like a kid herself. It surprised Jake. He'd never thought of his mom being unsure about anything. She always seemed to know so clearly what was right for her—and what she thought was right for him.

"Mom," Jake had said, trying to make his voice stronger for her. "Mom, you don't have to worry about me. I'm okay here for now. I'll just stay here. It's all right."

The conversation didn't end there, but that was all Jake remembered, aside from saying good-bye. Why had he said he was okay? He had never felt less okay in his whole life. But something had made him say those words, just as something made him know that he had to stay.

Jake quietly slipped his sneakers on. Kofi wasn't awake yet, although Muhammad had already stolen away to say his prayers. Jake walked over to the window, realizing perhaps for the first time how lucky he was that their room faced the sunrise. The first light was just beginning to turn the clouds pink as the door between the worlds started to open to let in the new day. As the Elder Brother, the Sun, began to show himself, the words from his dream repeated themselves even more clearly in his mind.

"Young warrior," the soft voice said again, "you have been called to do something. You have been called to help."

Jake realized that he had forgotten not only what he could do, but also what he had been given. And like that bird tap, tap, tapping on the window, the idea came fluttering back to him. This time, though, it no longer seemed as wild and foolish as it had at first. Now its wings were as wide as an eagle's. The only question that Jake still asked himself was whether or not he was really the one to do something like this. After all, he wasn't an elder, just an Indian kid.

Jake shook his head and clenched his fists.

No, that isn't the way to think, he told himself. He knew that part of his doubt was self-pity. Every person is equal in the eyes of the Creator. He needed not to think of himself as small and unimportant. He needed to think about what he could do for others. He had been given a gift.

"Remember," Grampa had said to him. And Jake remembered. "When you are given a gift, it is meant to be shared." The struggle in Jake's mind lasted only a few heartbeats. He knew what he had to do.

He turned back toward the room. Kofi was awake, sitting on his bed.

"I've got an idea," Jake said. "Listen." And then the words came pouring out of him. At first Kofi just listened, sitting and nodding. By the time Jake had finished, Kofi was on his feet.

"Jake," Kofi said, "you are wonderful. Come, you must do this. We must start telling people."

CHAPTER FIFTEEN
ALL PLAY

JAKE LOOKED AROUND THE LACROSSE FIELD. Dr. Marshall, who was holding his goalie's stick as if it were a baseball bat, nodded at him from where he stood by the eastern goal. It was still hard to believe that they had listened to him.

Earlier that morning, Jake had explained his idea to John, Darris, and Doug, the team captains. The three young men spoke to the other Weltimore Warriors. After everyone had agreed, the whole team went to Dr. Marshall's office.

"What can I do for you, boys?" Dr. Marshall asked. His voice seemed smaller, softer, and less certain than usual. His face looked drawn and tired.

"Jake can tell you," Doug said.

Then Jake spoke. He spoke without thinking of what he was going to say. He just let the words flow from his mouth, just as Grampa Sky had told him people did when they spoke in the old way, letting the Good Mind guide them, letting himself be a channel for the message.

"We want to play a game for Coach Scott," Jake said. "Not just a regular game, but a special one. We want to do it in the old Iroquois way, so that it brings all of our minds together for him, so that it becomes a prayer for him to get well. Anyone who wants to play could be part of it, not just the kids on the team."

Dr. Marshall's face had changed as Jake continued to speak, explaining how each time the ball went from one end of the field to the other, it was like the sun crossing the sky, like a day of healing passing under the eye of the Creator. Jake knew that his words, spoken from the heart, were touching the headmaster's heart. Dr. Marshall's eyes became moist, and Jake was unashamed of the tears in his own eyes as he spoke. But Jake's voice stayed strong and when he finished, Dr. Marshall reached out and took his hand.

"Young man," Dr. Marshall had said, "I can't think of a better thing for us to do. I have only one question."

"Sir?" Jake asked.

"May I play?"

Now Jake looked around the field, looked at each face. Dr. Marshall, Thomas Jones, the school security guard, and four of other teachers at Weltimore stood on the field, along with all the members of the Weltimore lacrosse team and as many students as they could find lacrosse sticks for. Kofi was there, and Muhammad. As Jake's eyes found them, both roommates flashed him a smile. Kofi tapped his heart with his hand and then made the peace sign toward him.

Around the field were more people than Jake had ever seen before at a Weltimore game. Surrounding the field were the rest of the student body, the faculty, the grounds' crew, and the administrative staff. Only one day had passed since Dr. Marshall had accepted their proposal to play a special game for Coach Scott, but word had spread. Lacrosse fans from all around the area, and even two TV crews, showed up.

All of this is good, Jake thought. *There is nothing secret about this. The more people who are here, the better.* Jake understood that as long as their thoughts were for Coach Scott, as long as they knew why this game was being played, it was good. Despite the size of the crowd, only a soft murmur could be heard, like the summer wind, rippling through the throng as people reverently whispered to each other.

Everyone was looking at Jake. *It's not as if they are looking at me,* Jake thought. *It's just that they want to know what to do next. They want to do the right thing.*

Jake walked to the center of the field and raised his lacrosse stick toward the sun. He waited as all the others on the field did the same, coming together in the center, lifting all of their sticks high.

"Today we play the Creator's game for Coach Scott," Jake said, loudly enough for all to hear.

"FOR COACH SCOTT," everyone repeated, their lacrosse sticks clacking together.

The game was like no other game Jake had ever played before. Somehow he knew that this was what it was like when the heart of every player was truly in the game. The ball seemed to join the game itself, moving across the field like a white bird in flight. Everyone played as hard as he would in any game. Despite the fact that so many players were on the field, it didn't feel awkward. Instead, there was a sweet flow to things, a surprising grace to it all.

Jake noticed two things that surprised him. One was how well Dr. Marshall, despite his small size and his round body, played in the goal. The headmaster even knew the vocabulary of the goalie, shouting, "Clear the crease!" and "Move out, Doug!" Another was that Thomas Jones had clearly played lacrosse before—and still played it very well. In fact, Mr. Jones scored the first goal, with an overhand shot that whizzed past Dr. Marshall.

After that first goal, the crowd was no longer hushed. People began to shout and wave their arms. Jake noticed that, for the first time since he'd played at Weltimore, everyone cheered for every good play. Each goal that was scored brought a roar from the whole crowd, no matter which side of the field it was on.

It had been agreed that the game would be played until a total of seven goals was reached. Already, four had been scored on the sunrise goal and two on the sunset. Now Jake had the ball. He stepped right, cradling his stick in both hands, planted, and spun left. The goal was open before him. But he didn't shoot. Instead, he tossed the ball to the player who stood across from him, on the other side of the goal. Muhammad held up his stick and caught the ball. Then, with a hockey player's underhand flick of his wrists, he shot. The ball went into the net.

Muhammad held up his racket in triumph. Jake did the same, followed by all of the others on the field. Without a bit of hesitation, the spectators ran onto the field. Several embraced Muhammad, who was smiling broadly, and others slapped Jake on the back, high-fiving him and the other players, who were hugging each other. It was as if everyone had been playing the game, as if everyone had won and no one had lost.

"Jake," said a familiar voice behind him. "Jakey."

Jake turned around. It was his mother.

"Mom!" he said. "You finally came to one of my games." Jake shook his head in surprise. "But how did you get here?"

Then his mother's arms surrounded him, and her lips brushed against his ear. "Jakey, I'm sorry I've been away so much. But there is no way I would have missed this game. I am so proud of you," she whispered. "I have never been so proud."

CHAPTER SIXTEEN

A WARRIOR'S HOME

"YOU CAN GO IN NOW," the nurse said.

Jake ran his hands over his hair. He made sure his school blazer was buttoned, and he straightened the knot in his tie one more time. Then he stepped into the room.

He thought he had been prepared, but when he saw how thin and pale Coach Scott looked, he couldn't help drawing in a breath before biting his lip.

Coach Scott saw his reaction and laughed. It wasn't much of a laugh, and Jake could tell that Coach Scott knew it.

"Mr. Forrest," Coach Scott said in a small, raspy voice, "come on . . . over here. Hard to . . . talk loud . . . with one collapsed lung." He straightened out his right index finger, lifted it, and then placed it on his chest. "First slug . . . went right . . . in here."

Then Coach Scott closed his eyes. Jake couldn't tell if he had gone back to sleep or if he just didn't want to talk anymore. The nurse had told him that with all the medication Coach was on, Jake's visit would have to be short. Coach Scott had been shot three times, and he had almost died. Somehow he had pulled through, but it would be months before he was well and strong again. Jake started to turn to leave.

Coach Scott's eyes opened. "Jake," he said. "Come here." He held out his hand, and Jake stepped forward to take it. Coach Scott held onto his hand, not the way someone takes a hand to shake it, but the way a person grabs on when he wants to be pulled back to safety. Coach Scott pulled, and Jake let himself be drawn in closer so that his face was close to the coach's.

"Some stunt . . . you pulled," Coach Scott rasped. "That game . . . you . . . set up."

"Unh-hunh," Jake said.

"Thought I knew all . . . there was . . . to know about our game. About our . . . beautiful game." Coach Scott said. He closed his eyes, then opened them and looked at Jake with eyes that were more wide-awake than before.

When he spoke, for just a moment, his voice had some of the strength Jake remembered. "Jake," he said, "I saw it all."

"You mean on TV?" Jake asked. "There were two stations that covered it."

Coach Scott lifted his chin a little toward the TV on the wall, then he shook his head. "Jake, I don't know how to say it. They turned on that TV for me to watch it, but when the game started it was as if I was there. Not in this room. There. I was on that field. Son, . . . son, . . . it helped me. No way to explain it. But I think you understand."

Jake nodded. There was no need to speak, not even to say "unh-hunh."

Coach Scott leaned back and closed his eyes, still speaking. "You tell . . . everyone I'm . . . going to be okay." His voice faded, becoming softer, more distant. "You tell them all . . . all my warriors . . . I said . . . thank you."

Jake waited, but Coach Scott had settled back into sleep. His breathing was gentle. His face looked peaceful. Jake carefully removed his hand from the coach's grasp.

He stood for a moment in the doorway, looking

back, thinking about how strange it was that things could change so quickly—the way he saw other people, the way he felt about a place, even the way he felt about himself. It all could be transformed so suddenly.

But Jake also knew there were some things that would always be true. One was that wherever he went, the Creator's game would be there for him. It truly was just like a prayer, reminding him of who he really was, reminding him to always be mindful and thankful. He would try hard never to forget that again. It was just as Grampa Sky had said to him, "As long as you remember and remain thankful, you can find peace in your heart."

He thought about what his mother had told him. It was all up to him now. He could decide where he wanted to live. Jake wasn't sure yet what he would decide. He could go back home, stay with Uncle Irwin and Aunt Alice, and be back at the Nation School with his old friends. But he had friends here at Weltimore, too. Now that the decision was his to make, Jake no longer felt trapped. Now he knew that a true warrior's home is not just the earth he walks upon. A true warrior's home is always in his heart.

About the Author

JOSEPH BRUCHAC was born in Saratoga Springs, New York, and grew up in the Adirondack foothills. He began to take an interest in his Abenaki heritage when he was a teenager. Mr. Bruchac has written many books, poems, plays, and short stories—many of which include tales, characters, and teachings from his Native American roots. Performing as a storyteller allows him another way to preserve his Abenaki culture.

Some of Mr. Bruchac's best-known children's and young adult books include *Skeleton Man*, *The Winter People*, *How Chipmunk Got His Stripes*, and a picture book about lacrosse, *The Great Ball Game*.

Mr. Bruchac and his wife Carol live in Greenfield Center, New York.